W9-BTC-699

THE MISSING TARTS

THE MISSING TARTS

STORY BY
B. G. Hennessy

PICTURES BY
Tracey Campbell Pearson

VIKING KESTREL

The artwork for each painting consists of an ink, watercolor, and
gouache painting that was camera separated and reproduced in full color.

VIKING KESTREL

Published by the Penguin Group
Viking Penguin Inc., 40 West 23rd Street, New York, New York 10010, U.S.A.
Penguin Books Ltd, 27 Wrights Lane, London W8 5TZ, England
Penguin Books Australia Ltd, Ringwood, Victoria, Australia
Penguin Books Canada Ltd, 2801 John Street, Markham, Ontario, Canada L3R 1B4
Penguin Books (N.Z.) Ltd, 182–190 Wairau Road, Auckland 10, New Zealand

Penguin Books Ltd, Registered Offices: Harmondsworth, Middlesex, England

First published in 1989 by Viking Penguin Inc.
Published simultaneously in Canada
1 3 5 7 9 10 8 6 4 2
Text copyright © B. G. Hennessy, 1989
Illustrations copyright © Tracey Campbell Pearson, 1989
All rights reserved

Library of Congress Cataloging-in-Publication Data
Hennessy, B. G. (Barbara G.) The missing tarts / by B. G. Hennessy;
illustrated by Tracey Campbell Pearson. p. cm.
Summary: When the Queen of Hearts discovers that her strawberry tarts have been stolen,
she enlists the help of many popular nursery rhyme characters in order to find them.
ISBN 0-670-82039-3 [1. Kings, queens, rulers, etc.—Fiction. 2. Characters and characteristics
in literature—Fiction.] I. Pearson, Tracey Campbell, ill. II Title.
PZ7.H3914Mi 1989 [E]—dc19 88-28809 CIP AC

Printed in Hong Kong by Imago Publishing Ltd.
Set in Berkeley Medium.

The Queen of Hearts
She made some tarts
All on a summer's day.
The Knave of Hearts
He stole those tarts
And took them clean away.

"Where are the tarts?"
asked the Queen of Hearts.

"Let's look up the hill," said Jack and Jill.

"Not in my bowl," said Old King Cole.

"Check the cupboard,"
said Old Mother Hubbard.

"Ask the cat," said Jack Sprat.

"Not in my corner,"
said Little Jack Horner.

"Follow that sheep," said
Little Bo Peep.

"Here's a clue!" said Little Boy Blue.

"You'll find them soon," said the Man in the Moon.

"They can't be far," twinkled the star.

The Queen of Hearts
She found those tarts
All on a summer's day.
The Knave of Hearts
Who took the tarts
Had given them all away!

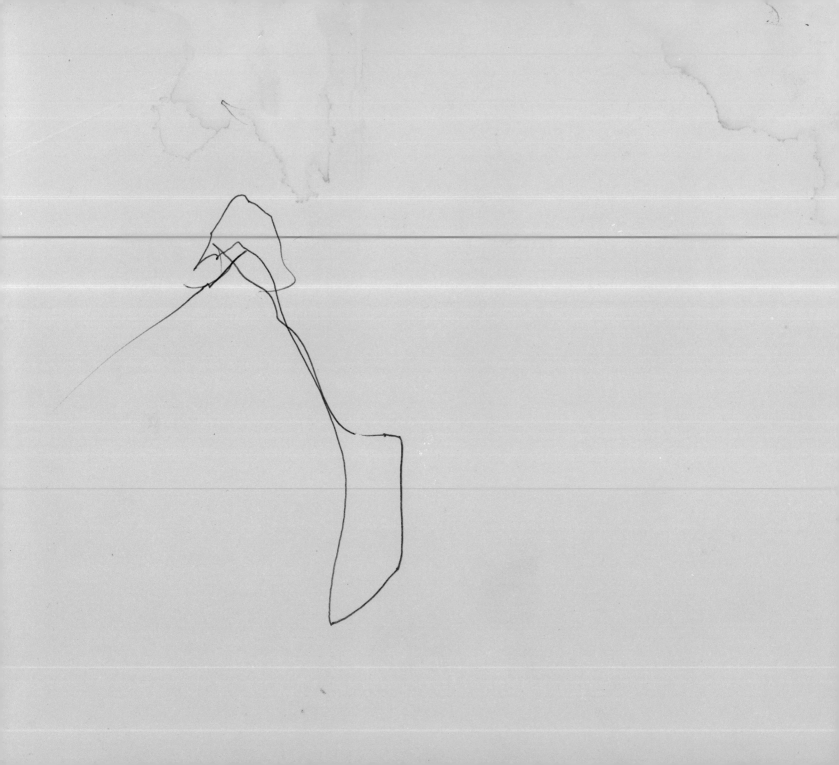